THE SPOILS OF WAR

© 2008 Weldon Owen Education Inc. All rights reserved.

No part of this publication may be reproduced or transmitted
in any form or by any means, electronic or mechanical,
including photocopying, recording, taping, or any information storage
and retrieval system, without permission in writing from the publisher.

Library of Congress Cataloging-in-Publication Data

Kenney, Karen Latchana.
 The Spoils of war / by Karen Latchana Kenney.
    p. cm. -- (Shockwave)
 Includes index.
 ISBN-10: 0-531-17757-2 (lib. bdg.)
 ISBN-13: 978-0-531-17757-0 (lib. bdg.)
 ISBN-10: 0-531-18837-X (pbk.)
 ISBN-13: 978-0-531-18837-8 (pbk.)
1. War and civilization--Juvenile literature. 2. War and society--Juvenile literature.
3. War--Psychological aspects--Juvenile literature. 4. Weapons of mass destruction--
Juvenile literature. I. Title. II. Series.

 CB481.K455 2008
 303.6'6--dc22

2007021670

Published in 2008 by Children's Press, an imprint of Scholastic Inc.,
557 Broadway, New York, New York 10012
www.scholastic.com

SCHOLASTIC, CHILDREN'S PRESS, and associated logos are trademarks
and/or registered trademarks of Scholastic Inc.

08 09 10 11 12 13 14 15 16 17
10 9 8 7 6 5 4 3 2 1

Printed in China through Colorcraft Ltd., Hong Kong

Author: Karen Latchana Kenney
Educational Consultant: Ian Morrison
Editor: Lynette Evans
Designer: Steve Clarke
Photo Researcher: Jamshed Mistry

Photographs by: Getty Images (p. 3; p. 14; explosion, p. 15; aerial spraying, p. 17); **Jennifer and Brian Lupton** (teenagers, pp. 32–33); **Photolibrary** (p. 7; fire, pp. 18–19); **Tranz/Corbis** (cover; pp. 8–9; pp. 11–13; anti-war protest, p. 15; aid to orphans, p. 17; tank, p. 18; man with bird, p.19; Jody Williams, sniffer dog, p. 21; pp. 22–23; p. 25; Doctors Without Borders, p. 27; pp. 28–29; Afghan girl, pp. 30–31; peacekeeper, pp. 32–33); **Tranz/Reuters** (p. 10; p. 16; landmine victim, pp. 20–21; p. 24; p. 26; Kofi Annan and Carla Del Ponte, p. 31)

All illustrations and other photographs © Weldon Owen Education Inc.

SHOCKWAVE
SOCIAL STUDIES

THE SPOILS OF WAR

Karen Latchana Kenney

children's press®
An imprint of Scholastic Inc.
NEW YORK • TORONTO • LONDON • AUCKLAND • SYDNEY
MEXICO CITY • NEW DELHI • HONG KONG
DANBURY, CONNECTICUT

CHECK THESE OUT!

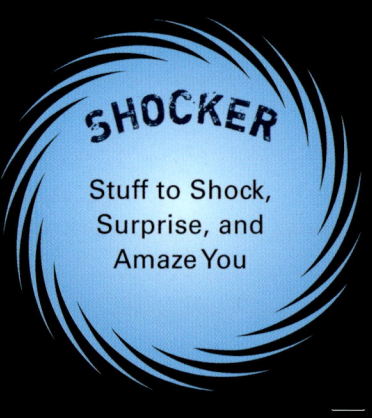

SHOCKER
Stuff to Shock, Surprise, and Amaze You

Quick Recaps and Notable Notes

Word Stunners and Other Oddities

The Heads-Up on Expert Reading

Links to More Information

CONTENTS

HIGH-POWERED WORDS	6
GET ON THE WAVELENGTH	8

War and Peace	10
A Global War	12
Sticky Fire	14
Agent Orange	16
Environmental Warfare	18
Hidden Bombs	20
Living in a War Zone	22
Refugee Camps	24
Relief Organizations	26
Returning Home	28
Reconstruction and Healing	30

AFTERSHOCKS	32
GLOSSARY	34
FIND OUT MORE	35
INDEX	36
ABOUT THE AUTHOR	36

HIGH-POWERED WORDS

aftermath the period immediately following a terrible event such as a war or a natural disaster

allies a group of nations that unite with each other for a common goal

atomic bomb a nuclear weapon that gets its explosive power from the splitting of atoms

humanitarian (*hyoo man uh TEHR ee uhn*) devoted to caring for others and improving their lives

land mine an explosive placed just under the surface of the ground and designed to explode when the weight of a person or a vehicle passes over it

negotiate (*ni GOH shee ate*) to discuss with the intention of reaching an agreement

refugee a person who is forced to leave his or her home because of war, persecution, or a natural disaster

For additional vocabulary, see Glossary on page 34.

The word *aftermath* comes from Old English. *Math* referred to "mowing." So originally, *aftermath* referred to "a second cut of grass, after harvesting the first."

Millions of **land mines** are buried in war-torn countries, such as Cambodia. Land mines are difficult and very dangerous to remove.

There is a famous quote that says, "to the victor belong the spoils." Battles have always been fought, and they have been fought for many reasons. War is the deliberate and organized use of violence between political groups. It is usually the last, drastic step after opposing sides have tried to solve their **conflicts** in a peaceful way. Sometimes wars are fought because two groups disagree over who should own resources, such as land, water, energy supplies, or minerals. Sometimes wars are fought because two groups have differing ideas about religion or governance, for example.

People fled Kosovo, in Europe in 1999, as unrest grew. **NATO** sent thousands of tanks and forces in an effort to manage the crisis peacefully.

In war, the winning side might assume that its win gives it the right to any "treasure" from the defeated. These treasures are one example of "the spoils of war." However, victory in war comes with more than profit for the winning side. It comes with responsibility. The winners of a war are responsible for helping survivors rebuild their lives, homes, and nations.

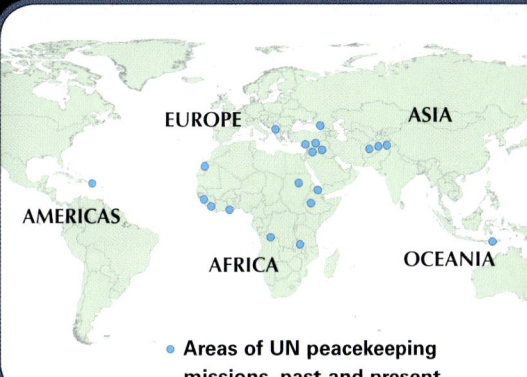

• Areas of UN peacekeeping missions, past and present

THE UNITED NATIONS

The United Nations (UN) is an organization of nations that work together to try to solve problems through peaceful means. The UN works to settle disagreements before they lead to fighting.

Since its formation in 1945, the UN has run many peacekeeping operations around the world.

The United Nations' flag shows a map of the world surrounded by a wreath of olive branches, a symbol of peace.

War and Peace

Wars have been fought for many thousands of years. Some things about wars have not changed over time. All wars cause suffering and hardship. All wars cost lives and money. They require large numbers of soldiers, equipment, and weapons. They damage the environment. They destroy homes, families, and even nations.

However, the ways in which wars have been fought have changed over time as new technology in weaponry, transportation, and communication have become available. The rules of warfare, or the ways in which people are expected to behave during wartime, have also changed. Treaties, such as the **Geneva Convention**, have been drawn up, and the concept of **war crimes** has been established. The ways in which people try to recover and rebuild after wars have changed too. Today, peacekeeping forces, such as those run by the United Nations, and **humanitarian** organizations, such as the Red Cross, play an important role in the **aftermath** of war.

The Red Cross helps people who are the victims of war, hunger, or a natural disaster. Workers and donated supplies are identified by a red cross or, in Muslim countries, a red crescent on a white background.

A U.S. soldier carries an injured Iraqi boy to safety during a battle between U.S. and Iraqi forces in 2003.

Milestones of War and Peace

8000–6000 B.C.
- Soldiers use weapons such as swords, shields, and spears.

By 1400s
- Battles in Europe involve firearms such as guns and cannons.

Late 1800s–1900s
- Hague and Geneva Conventions provide rules about humane behavior during war.

1914–1918: World War I
- Airplanes and submarines are used.

1920–1946
- League of Nations is formed to maintain peace among nations.

1939–1945: World War II
- Atomic bomb is dropped.

1945
- United Nations is formed to establish peace and security.

Soldiers in UN peacekeeping forces wear their own national uniforms. They also wear blue hats, helmets, or turbans with the UN symbol. This identifies them as UN peacekeepers.

The Cost of War
- suffering and hardship
- lives
- money
- homes destroyed
- families destroyed
- countries destroyed

A Global War

With the advance of technology, World War II took more lives and had more far-reaching consequences than any other war in history. Fighting began in Europe in 1939. The war expanded to include countries in Asia and the Pacific. From then on, the U.S. battled alongside its **allies** in both Europe and the Pacific. In 1941, Japanese aircraft bombed the U.S. naval base at Pearl Harbor, in Hawaii, causing the U.S. to battle fiercely with Japan. The war in Europe ended in May of 1945. U.S. President Harry Truman wanted to end the conflict with Japan as well. He made the difficult decision to use a new weapon, the **atomic bomb**.

When the United States dropped atomic bombs on the Japanese cities of Hiroshima and Nagasaki in 1945, there was a blinding flash followed by a shockwave. The two cities were destroyed. More than 100,000 people died instantly, thousands of buildings fell, and hospitals were knocked down. In the weeks that followed, survivors got **radiation** sickness. This was the first time a nuclear weapon had been used in war. Its full effects were unknown at the time. Five to ten years after the atomic bomb, however, survivors began to develop cancer from the radiation.

George Marshall was chief of staff of the U.S. Army during World War II. He proposed a plan, called the Marshall Plan, to help rebuild post-war Europe. Billions of U.S. dollars were put to this cause, and in 1953 Marshall was awarded a Nobel Peace Prize for his work. He is shown here with a group of cub scouts who presented him with their own "Junior Marshall Plan" in efforts to raise funds for children in Europe.

SHOCKER

It is not only people who would be horribly affected by a worldwide nuclear war. The term *nuclear winter* refers to the deadly global environmental effects to be expected in the event of such a conflict.

Atomic bomb exploding in Nagasaki

PATH TO PEACE

In 1945, Japan surrendered because of the terrible destruction caused by the atomic bombs. Immediately after the bombs were dropped, the United States provided medical supplies and food packages. Allied forces took control of Japan and disarmed millions of Japanese troops. They took steps to guide Japan toward democracy. Allied occupation ended in 1952. Relations between Japan and the United States were restored.

In 1953, the Japan–U.S. Treaty of Friendship, Commerce, and Navigation was signed. This treaty promoted economic and cultural ties between the two countries. In 1956, Japan was admitted as a member of the United Nations. Economic ties between the United States and Japan have since grown strong. Today, the two countries are allies. They share visions and goals for a better future.

I have seen programs about both Pearl Harbor and the atomic bomb, so I already know something about this topic. Making connections sure makes reading easier.

Sticky Fire

By the time of the Vietnam War (1959–1975), technology had produced other deadly inventions. During this conflict, the allies of North Vietnam fought the government and allies of South Vietnam. South Vietnam's chief ally was the United States. Thickly forested areas throughout Vietnam provided hiding places for fighters on both sides. Fire bombs were used to clear forests. **Napalm** (a gasoline gel) was used to make the fire stick to surfaces. The fire burned longer, sucking oxygen from the air, and suffocating people. Airplanes flying over the targeted areas dropped napalm bombs. The sticky **substance** stuck to the leaves of plants. It destroyed forests and food crops. The fires forced people and animals to flee.

The aftereffects of napalm use were extensive. Besides the human cost, napalm devastated the landscape and disrupted ecosystems for years to come. Huge craters were burned into the land, ruining topsoil, killing animals, and destroying habitats.

Phan Thi Kim Phuc is a living symbol of the suffering of innocent **civilians** during wartime. When she was nine years old, her village in Vietnam was bombed with napalm. She was so badly burned that no one expected her to survive. Today, Phan Thi Kim Phuc devotes her life to promoting peace. She is shown here with her baby son.

SHOCKER

The large-scale destruction of vegetation during the war in Vietnam greatly affected wildlife in the area. Two rare species of ibis are now believed to be extinct.

Napalm is a blended word (sometimes called a portmanteau word). It is made up of two words: *naphthene* and *palmitate*. Other blended words include: *motel* (*motor* and *hotel*); *smog* (*smoke* and *fog*); and *swipe* (*sweep* and *wipe*).

Napalm bombs exploding in fields south of Saigon during the Vietnam War

CHEMICAL WEAPONS BANNED

The destruction caused by napalm led to the creation of an organization that aimed to prevent napalm's use ever again. The Organization for the Prohibition of Chemical Weapons was formed in 1997. Its purpose has been to eliminate all chemical weapons and their use. Teams of workers supervise the destruction of stored chemical weapons. The organization also polices nations in an attempt to prevent the creation of new weapons.

VOICES OF PROTEST

The support of its people on the homefront is one of the most important resources the military has. During the Vietnam War, the U.S. had superior weapons and military power. However, at home, huge numbers of U.S. citizens opposed the war. Millions of protesters took to the streets. As a result, the U.S. government eventually withdrew its troops and **negotiated** for peace.

Agent Orange

Napalm was not the only deadly chemical used during the Vietnam War. In Operation Ranch Hand, 19 million gallons of **herbicide** were sprayed over the land. The herbicide was called Agent Orange because it was stored in barrels with orange stripes. Like napalm, it wiped out food sources for enemy soldiers and revealed enemy hiding places by destroying jungle. The **toxic** chemicals in Agent Orange **contaminated** soil and seeped into water supplies.

Agent Orange had terrible and long-lasting effects on people. Those exposed have suffered many illnesses. Adults who came into contact with Agent Orange have given birth to children with limbs and body parts that are malformed or missing. Many of these children have been abandoned at orphanages throughout Vietnam.

Today, organizations throughout the world help provide care, support, homes, and families for Vietnam's orphans. They work hard to improve health care, education, and quality of life for children in the orphanages.

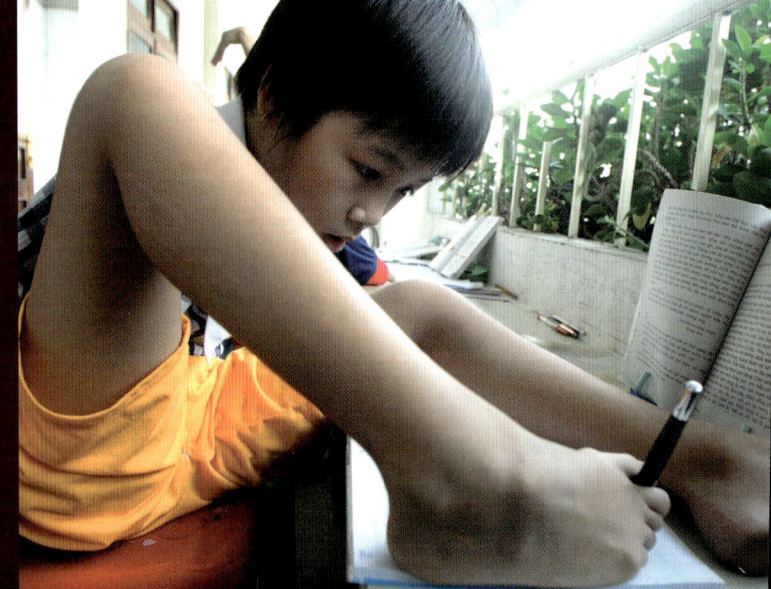

Ten-year-old Pham Thi Thuy Linh has learned to write with her foot. She was born in southern Vietnam, where Agent Orange was sprayed during the war. She was born without arms. She is shown here at the Peace Village in Tu Du hospital in Ho Chi Minh City, Vietnam.

FOUNDATIONS FOR SUPPORT

Charity groups from around the world raise money and donate medical supplies, school supplies, time, and labor to help brighten the lives of orphans and children with disabilities in Vietnam. The boy shown below looks at art supplies given to him by U.S. veterans who often visit orphanages in Vietnam as members of an organization called Vets With a Mission.

RETURNING HOME

Thirty years ago, Jonathan Groth (below left) was one of 30,000 orphans flown out of Vietnam at the end of the war in a mission called Operation Babylift. Jonathan is now a U.S. citizen. He recently spent time with children at an orphanage in Ho Chi Minh City.

The *mal* in *malformed* means "ill" or "badly." Similar words are *malady*, *malnutrition*, and *malaria* (bad air).

Environmental Warfare

Exploding bombs and chemical weapons are not the only forces that do damage to the environment during war. Tanks and armored trucks carrying soldiers and supplies compact the soil and kill delicate plants. Toxic, radioactive waste left from detonated bombs can also have devastating effects. This waste has often been dumped into oceans.

Oil was used as a weapon during the Persian Gulf War in 1990 and 1991. This war began when Iraq invaded Kuwait. As many as 630 wells in Kuwait were deliberately set on fire by Iraqi soldiers. Black smoke filled the air for months. In a second act of environmental warfare, millions of gallons of oil were pumped into the Persian Gulf. The oil killed seabirds and marine wildlife.

After the war, local and international teams arrived to clean up. People removed oil from the surface of the water and tried to clean the shorelines. Firefighting teams put out the oil-well fires. The U.S. Environmental Protection Agency (EPA) supplied special equipment to monitor air pollution in the region.

SHOCKER

Sound waves have been used by the U.S. navy to detect submarines in the ocean. These sonar blasts are thought to be causing whales to beach themselves and die.

SAVING WILDLIFE

Oil floats on water and usually spreads out quickly over the surface to form a thin layer, known as an oil slick. During the Gulf War, the spilled oil killed tens of thousands of marine birds, sea turtles, and marine mammals. The Jubail Wildlife Rescue Project in Saudi Arabia saved many birds, turtles, and sea snakes from the oily Persian Gulf. People rescued animals and cleaned the oil off them at the center before returning them to the wild. Prince Abdullah al-Saud is shown here during a visit to the rescue center in 1991.

When I began reading the second paragraph, I thought I had made a mistake. How could oil be a weapon? So I reread the first sentence just to make sure I had it right. Rereading helps to confirm when you are right, as well as correct misconceptions.

Hidden Bombs

Another aftereffect of war remains hidden underground in as many as 70 countries around the world. Anything bigger than a rabbit can set off small explosives called **land mines**. These explosives have been used because they cost as little as $3 each to make, are easily buried, and have proved to be horribly effective. Land mines are often deadly, but they also cause many terrible, nonfatal injuries. Many people in countries affected by land mines lose arms or legs in the blasts. They need **prosthetic** limbs or wheelchairs in order to move around.

Land mines are banned today, largely because of the work of Jody Williams, who organized an International Campaign to Ban Landmines (ICBL). However, much hard work remains. Land mines are costly and very dangerous to remove. It is thought that approximately 60 million remain buried.

SHOCKER

Every month, more than 2,000 people are killed or injured by land-mine explosions. More than 70 percent of land-mine accidents involve civilians, many of whom are children.

LAND-MINE LOCATIONS

The map at right shows the countries in the world with the largest number of land mines yet to be removed and destroyed. In some cases, large areas of the country's farmland are unusable due to unexploded land mines.

Croatia
Bosnia
Iraq
Afghanistan
Sudan
Eritrea
Cambodia
Somalia
Mozambique

CYBER CAMPAIGN

Jody Williams received the 1997 Nobel Peace Prize for her work to ban land mines. The ICBL treaty was signed by 122 nations. From her home in the United States, Williams sent hundreds of e-mails to countries around the world, convincing them to join her campaign.

THE SMELL OF DANGER

The Marshall Legacy Institute (MLI) is an organization that started the K9 Demining (de-mining) Program. This program trains dogs to sniff out land mines. Most land mines have only small amounts of metal. They are difficult to locate with a metal detector. Mine-detection dogs are trained to locate the scent of explosives. They alert a handler to mark the exact spot. The mine is then removed or destroyed safely.

Living in a War Zone

For three years, bombs and bullets rained down on the city of Sarajevo, in southeastern Europe. Conflict began brewing there in 1991, when the country of Yugoslavia began to separate into smaller states. Different **ethnic** and religious groups in Bosnia, which had been part of Yugoslavia, disagreed over whether Bosnia should become independent of Yugoslavia. By 1992, the capital city, Sarajevo, was plunged into war. Buildings were destroyed beneath the bombs and bullets, and people went into hiding. Some sheltered in cellars. The lucky ones escaped the city.

As members of NATO-led peacekeeping forces, U.S. soldiers played an important role in protecting citizens during the conflict. However, as many as 20,000 people died during the war in Bosnia-Herzegovina. In 1995, warring sides agreed to a peace plan. Peace negotiations took place in Dayton, Ohio. Today, people are still working to repair the damage and keep the peace.

UN peacekeepers also played an important part in helping the wounded during the war in Bosnia. Here they help a man who was injured after a bomb exploded in the main market square of Sarajevo.

Events in Bosnia

1991: Yugoslavia begins to break up. Different ethnic groups disagree.

1992: Sarajevo plunges into war.

By 1995: Approximately 20,000 people have died in the fighting.

Today: People still work to keep peace.

A line of traffic forms as citizens of Sarajevo attempt to flee the violence in the city.

THE POWER OF THE PEN

Zlata Filipovic was ten years old when she decided to keep a diary of her carefree life in Sarajevo. At the time, she had no idea that she and her parents would soon be hiding from exploding bombs. Zlata kept up with her diary throughout the war. She wrote about the food shortages. She wrote about the boredom of being stuck indoors because of gunfire. She wrote about friends leaving or being injured. Her diary has since been translated into many languages.

SURVIVORS' STORYTELLER

War brought a sudden end to the childhood of a fifteen-year-old boy named Elie Wiesel in 1944. During World War II, Nazi soldiers removed entire communities of Jewish people living in areas of Europe. Elie was separated from his mother and sister and, with his father, sent to **concentration camps**. Somehow Elie survived the horrors of the camps. He later wrote books and plays about the **Holocaust**. In 1986, his work earned him the Nobel Prize for Peace.

Refugee Camps

Millions of people can become displaced as a result of war. Some flee to safety in other countries to escape the violence and unfair treatment in their own country. They become **refugees**. Others move to a safer part of their country. They become what are known as Internally Displaced Persons (IDPs). By the end of World War II, there were about 12 million displaced persons in Europe. Many of them lived permanently in camps.

This is not simply a problem of the past, however. In 2004, about 25 million people became IDPs. An estimated 9.2 million refugees from various countries around the world were forced to flee their homelands due to war. Until very recently, many people have fled **civil war** in the African countries of Sudan, Rwanda, and Chad. Refugees and IDPs often travel in huge numbers to camps, where conditions are usually poor. Families live in tents or shacks. Water and good sources of food are scarce. Overcrowding and lack of **sanitation** cause disease. Lacking security, the camps are often dangerous.

Thousands of refugees fled war and drought in Afghanistan in 2001. The World Food Program tried to distribute emergency aid to refugees at this camp in Jallozai, Pakistan, where approximately 70,000 people were living in makeshift tents.

FOR THE CHILDREN

Children make up a large part of the population in refugee camps. It was estimated that 114,000 children were orphaned, abandoned, or lost during a violent civil war in the African nation of Rwanda in 1994 alone.

There are several organizations that help children. The United Nations Children's Fund (UNICEF) was formed after World War II to provide food, clothing, and medical supplies for children who are victims of war. Save the Children and other organizations have worked to create a standard way to collect data and trace children's families.

Doctors Without Borders, also called Médecins Sans Frontières (MSF), provides medical care at many refugee camps around the world. Here an MSF doctor treats a child at a camp for Hutu and Tutsi refugees from Rwanda.

A crowd of Hutu refugees from Rwanda shelter at Benaco Refugee Camp in Tanzania, 1994.

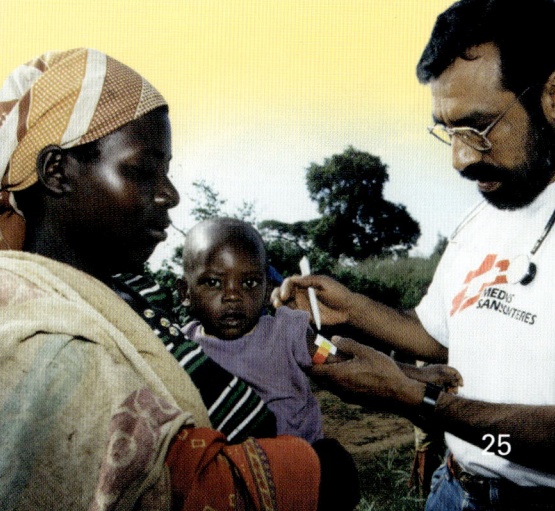

Relief Organizations

There are several relief organizations that provide medical care, food, water, and shelter for people who have suffered through war and disaster. Many of these are small, community-based groups. The Red Cross was one of the earliest humanitarian organizations. It was founded in 1863, in Switzerland. At first, the Red Cross gave medical aid only to soldiers. It was established as a neutral organization that could move freely around a battlefield, caring for the wounded. Today, many people donate time, skills, or money so that the Red Cross can help any people in need.

One of the most important goals of the United Nations is to help make the world a better and safer place in which to live. Providing various forms of aid is one way in which the UN works toward this goal. The UN itself receives funding from many of the world's wealthy nations. It assists developing countries with health care, education, and sanitation. It provides emergency food supplies and, in some cases, delivers food and medicine to war-torn countries.

As is the case with most humanitarian organizations, the Red Cross relies on volunteers for much of its work.

Doctors Without Borders (MSF) is a nonprofit organization that arranges relief in more than 80 countries each year. It was formed by a group of doctors in 1971. Thousands of doctors and other medical experts volunteer their skills.

Food packages often come from afar. The Hercules airplane is a useful packhorse. Its huge rear door makes it easy to load and unload cargo.

Returning Home

Coming home to family and friends can be a relief to a soldier, peacekeeper, aid worker, or anyone who has left home because of war. However, returning to a "normal life" is often difficult after living in a **traumatic** situation. Not only does war harm people physically, but the experiences people endure also affect their thoughts and actions. People can suffer from the experience of war long after their involvement has ended.

Veterans may return from war with strong feelings about what they witnessed, or the tasks they had to perform. Many feel jumpy or concerned for their safety. They may miss friends lost in **combat**. These feelings often affect their sleep. When they manage to fall asleep, they may relive combat events in nightmares. Anyone involved in war can suffer from depression and fear. These feelings are part of an ailment called Post Traumatic Stress Disorder (PTSD).

Many countries around the world set aside special days to remember soldiers who lost their lives during war. On these **memorial** days, people take part in parades and make speeches. Veterans Day is a holiday in the U.S. It is celebrated on November 11, which is the anniversary of the end of World War I (1914–1918). Many people donate money on memorial days. In return, they receive a paper poppy. This blood-red flower grew on battlefields in Europe. The donations are used to help veterans with disabilities.

HISTORY OF PTSD

Before the Vietnam War, little was known about PTSD. During World War I, soldiers who showed stress or anxiety after combat were referred to as being "shell-shocked." In World War II, this same condition was referred to as "combat fatigue."

In 1980, the American Psychological Association labeled these psychological effects of war PTSD, and called it an illness. This formally acknowledged the illness and allowed for treatments. The U.S. military now tries to prepare soldiers for the psychological effects of war.

The U.S. Department of Veteran Affairs has counseling centers set up around the country. Veterans who have experienced combat make up 60 percent of the staff at these centers. Counselors help veterans talk about their experiences and deal with the psychological aftermath of war.

Reconstruction and Healing

Civilians who witness their homes and the pattern of their everyday lives destroyed by war may understandably feel resentment or a need for revenge. It is traumatic to witness friends and family being hurt or killed. It is terrible to see your home, village, city, or nation destroyed. For healing to take place, people search to find ways to forgive and move on after war. Many try to reconcile their differences through peaceful means.

When war ends, a great deal of hard work needs to be done. Rebuilding a society may take years. Many organizations give humanitarian aid to help countries rebuild their **infrastructure** and restore buildings damaged by war. The safety and security of citizens, establishing a system of justice, and meeting basic needs, including health care and education, are important factors in the reconstruction process.

A young girl from Afghanistan, whose home was destroyed by war, stands in front of ruins in Kabul, the capital. Reconstruction is now underway.

LEADING THE WAY TO PEACE

Hundreds of years ago, a Native American man known as the Peacemaker proved that a cycle of violence and fighting could be ended. He brought five warring tribes together. Instead of fighting, they formed a league and pledged to work together. The group was called the Iroquois League. An eagle on top of the Tree of Peace is one symbol of the Iroquois League, which continues to this day.

HEALING THROUGH JUSTICE

Most nations have signed international treaties and agreements about the rules of war. These rules deal with issues such as the fair treatment of prisoners of war and the humane treatment of civilians during war. People who break these rules can be tried in court for war crimes. Here Swiss attorney Carla Del Ponte is shown with Kofi Annan – UN Secretary General – in 1999. She is being welcomed as the UN's chief prosecutor during a tribunal for war crimes committed during the war in former Yugoslavia.

AFTERSHOCKS

There are different kinds of wars. International wars are violent conflicts between two or more countries. Civil wars are violent conflicts between different political groups within one country. Revolutionary wars are violent conflicts between a government and a rebel group of the same country. Although wars vary and the reasons for fighting are diverse, all wars have life-changing consequences for the survivors.

WHAT DO YOU THINK?

In the aftermath of war, do the victors have a responsibility to help improve the lives of people in the defeated nation?

PRO

The victor has a duty to reconstruct a defeated nation after war. They should provide services, supplies, and whatever aid necessary to assist the people. Rebuilding helps make communities safe and stable. It helps prevent conflict from breaking out again.

For people who have survived war in their own country and are left to pick up the pieces and rebuild their lives, the presence of foreign military or peacekeeping forces can be either a blessing or a burden. Peacekeepers help establish law, order, and a return to safety. For some people, they might almost be heroes. For other people, their presence may serve as a painful reminder of lost lives and lost independence.

CON

Sometimes people don't want help from the victor. Sometimes the winner forces the people to adopt its culture and systems. If the people want to rebuild the nation in their own way, the winner should leave them alone.

GLOSSARY

civilian (*si VIL yuhn*) a person not in the armed services

civil war a war between two groups of people living in the same country

combat armed fighting against enemy forces

concentration camp a camp where people are imprisoned or killed for their race or beliefs, especially such a place controlled by Nazi Germany in World War II

conflict a fight, battle, or struggle

contaminate to make unfit for use

ethnic having to do with a group of people who share the same ancestors, customs, and laws

Geneva Convention a treaty signed in 1864 and still in effect, which provides rules on the humane treatment of people during wartime

herbicide a chemical used to destroy plants, especially weeds

Holocaust the mass slaughter of millions of European Jews and others by the Nazis during World War II

infrastructure the basic facilities serving a country, city, or area

memorial (*muh MOR ee uhl*) something that is built or done to help people continue to remember an event or a person who has died

napalm a jelly-like substance used to make fire bombs

NATO stands for North Atlantic Treaty Organization, and consists of more than 20 countries. NATO conducts peacekeeping missions and uses the military to protect its member countries.

prosthetic a device that substitutes for a part of the body that is missing or defective

radiation energy released from nuclear explosions, causing sickness and death

sanitation systems and facilities for keeping water clean and getting rid of sewage

substance a material that can be seen or weighed

toxic (*TOK sik*) poisonous

traumatic (*traw MAT ik*) something that is very upsetting, damaging, and shocking

war crime a crime committed against an enemy or a prisoner of war during wartime

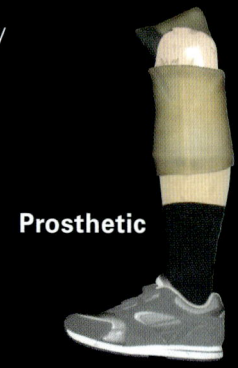

Prosthetic

FIND OUT MORE

BOOKS

Adams, Simon. *World War I*. DK Eyewitness, 2004.

Billings, Henry. *History of Our World: People, Places, and Ideas*. Steck-Vaughn 2003.

Bobrick, Benson. *Fight for Freedom: The American Revolutionary War*. Atheneum Books for Young Readers, 2004.

Children's History of the 20th Century. DK Children, 1999.

Goldstein, Margaret J. *World War II: Europe*. Lerner Publishing Group, 2004.

WEB SITES

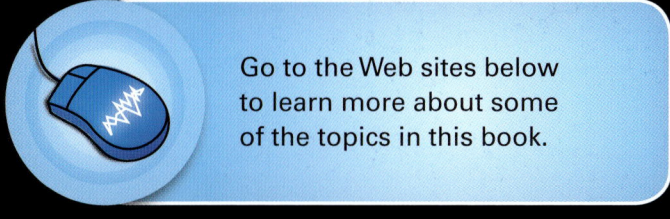

Go to the Web sites below to learn more about some of the topics in this book.

www.historyplace.com/unitedstates/vietnam/index.html

www.digitalhistory.uh.edu/modules/ww2

www.lewispublishing.com/faq.htm

www.youthambassadors.com/childrenandwar/landmines.html

http://news.nationalgeographic.com/kids/2004/11/refugees.html

INDEX

Agent Orange	16, 21	Red Cross	10, 26
Bosnia	22	refugees	24–25
children	11–14, 16–17, 20, 23, 25, 30	Rwanda	24–25
Doctors Without Borders	25, 27	treaties	10, 13, 20–21, 31
Japan	12–13	United Nations	9, 11, 13, 25–26, 31
land mines	20–21	veterans	17, 28–29
napalm	14–16, 21	Vietnam	14–17, 29
Persian Gulf War	18–19	World War I	11, 28–29
PTSD	28–29	World War II	11–13, 23

ABOUT THE AUTHOR

Karen Latchana Kenney is the author of several fiction and nonfiction books for children. She loves to learn about new things through reading and research. As an editor and writer, Karen gets to research various aspects of topics and learn about different groups of people from all over the world. While researching this book, she was impressed to find that many nonprofit organizations have formed to help people who have been affected by war.